# TAKING FLIGHT

By Adam Hancher

Frances Lincoln
Children's Books

It all began in a backyard in Dayton, Ohio when Bishop Milton Wright came home with a gift for his two boys.

"Wilbur! Orville!" he called.
"I have something for you!"

"What is it?" cried the brothers.

"It's a toy all the way from France. You won't believe what it can do!" he replied.

Slowly they wound up the propeller, and then let the toy go.

The brothers were mesmerised as it hung high in the air.

"One day, I'm going to fly, just like that!" said Orville.

"Not before I do!" said Wilbur.

Some years later, Wilbur
and Orville were hard at work.
This was no surprise. The brothers
were always hard at work.

They had built
paper-folding machines.

They had built printing presses.

And they built the *best* bicycles in Dayton!

WE HAVE THEM!

But their latest project was
by far the biggest...

The Wright brothers wanted to build a machine
that could fly, just as they had always dreamed.

"But where do we start?"
said Orville.

LILIENTHAL
TRAGEDY

$L = ksv^2C_l$

First, the brothers built a glider,
but it didn't have any control in the air.

"Well, how does a bird fly?"
asked Wilbur, watching as a goose glided
effortlessly through the sky.

"See how its wing twists?" said Orville.
"That's how it controls where it's going."

Then one afternoon, as Wilbur sat in the bicycle shop, idly twisting an empty box in his hand, the solution dawned on him.

"Orville!" he exclaimed,
"I've got it!"

And he had.

Using this idea, they built a wing that could twist, helping the glider to turn like a bird.

Now they needed somewhere to test out their new glider... somewhere windy, sandy and, above all, secret.

Out came the map.

Kitty Hawk, North Carolina, was one of the windiest places in the country.

Miles of sand dunes stretched out before them —
useful for a soft landing! —
and it was so perfectly quiet.

There was nothing here to stop
them from doing what they did best:

arguing,

experimenting

and inventing!

Wilbur tested the glider first.

He launched himself from the
top of a sand dune, and whilst Kitty
Hawk's strong winds did lift him up…

something was wrong, and he
thudded to the ground.

"Not in a thousand
years will man ever fly!"
said Wilbur, frustrated.

"I don't understand," said Orville, back in the workshop.

Puzzled, they decided to investigate, and built a special wind tunnel to test their designs.

After months of research the brothers had a new, improved glider.

It was time to return to Kitty Hawk.

"This time we *will* fly!" said Orville.

But their sister Katharine had something to say first.

"Remember what Father said: you mustn't fly together," she ordered. "What would happen if you both crashed? I don't have the time to nurse a pair of broken brothers!"

"Okay!" laughed Orville. "But we won't crash.

We've checked every inch of this glider and it's in top shape!"

"Let's see if it flies!" said Wilbur, and together they scaled the sand dune.

And fly it did!

Before too long, they
became confident pilots.

"Well, we can glide like a bird," said Wilbur later, "but now we need to power this thing!"

"We need an engine," said Wilbur, but no engine was light enough – or powerful enough.

"And we need propellers," said Orville, but nothing fitted their flyer.

"I guess we'll just have to build them ourselves," said Orville. "But we might need some help."

Luckily they knew just the man: Charlie Taylor, their most trusted bicycle mechanic.

Not long after, the brothers – with Charlie's expert help – had built a
flying machine that could take off and land under its own power.

They set off for Kitty Hawk once again, where they
found the curious coast guard waiting for them.

"Will it really be able to fly?" they asked, as they
eyed up the strange contraption.

"There's one way to find out!" said Orville.

A freezing wind blew…

And Orville flew straight into it!

Everyone gasped as he soared overhead.
The men below had witnessed the first brief journey of a
Wright flying machine. One even managed to photograph the event!

The brothers flew again and again, taking turns to test their machine.

"That time you were up for 59 seconds!" called Orville. "You flew 852 feet."

"That was just the beginning!" shouted Wilbur.

And it was! But the Wright brothers had competition – aviators all around the world were chasing the same dream.

The race was on!

While others made flight attempts in front of huge crowds, the Wright brothers worked in secret to perfect their machine, and almost no one saw them fly for another two years. So when news began to spread about their flights, few people could believe it.

"Liars!" said the newspapers in America. "Bluffeurs!" said the doubters in Europe.

"Why don't you show them what you can do?" Charlie asked.
"Our flyer is as good as anybody's, but no one will believe that
you can fly until you prove it."

But the brothers stayed patient. They were waiting for
just the right moment to reveal their machine.

Finally, in 1908, they were ready.

"No more secrecy," said Orville. "No more doubters.

It's time to fly in front of all the world!"

The brothers had a plan.

Wilbur set sail for France, where the intrigued crowds in Europe awaited him, while Orville travelled with Charlie and Katharine to Fort Myer to show off their machine to the military.

"Can you carry a passenger?" the officials asked Orville,
and Lieutenant Thomas E. Selfridge stepped forward.
"Well, it's now or never!" thought Orville as the two men prepared
to fly. "Nine years of hard work… and now they'll see."

Orville took off, and the astonished crowd watched him
soar higher and higher— but something was wrong.

A propeller snapped.
    The flyer spiralled out of control,
        and the two men plummeted to earth,
            smashing onto the ground.

Orville was terribly hurt.
Poor Lieutenant Selfridge did not survive the crash.

"I always feared this would happen!"
said Katharine, rushing to her brother's side.

But nothing could keep Orville down!
Katharine soon had him back on his feet, and before long,
they were on their way to see Wilbur in France.

"Don't think I've sat here waiting
idly, Orv!" said Wilbur.

In fact Wilbur had been very
busy indeed.

While Orville
recovered, Wilbur
had continued to fly
and had broken
many records.

No one had seen a machine fly with such control! Cutting through the air
in figures of eight, he twisted and turned, delighting the crowd.

"Wilbur Wright and his great white bird, the beautiful mechanical bird!" the people
proclaimed. The brothers were back in the news, but now it was for all the right reasons.
Their fame soon spread around the world…

And so, putting disaster behind them, Orville and Wilbur
watched their childhood dreams finally taking flight,

and these two humble brothers from Dayton
became the heroes of the skies.

Orville (left), 1874 and
Wilbur (right), 1876.

Orville (left), Katharine and
Wilbur (right), 1900.

Test flight of
the Wright
Glider, 1902

Memorial tower at
Kill Devil Hill, built
on the site of the
Kitty Hawk sand
dunes visited by the
Wright Brothers,
dedicated in 1932.

# The Wright Brothers' lives and legacy

Wilbur Wright was born on 16 April 1867, followed by Orville Wright on 19 August 1871. In 1892, the brothers opened their famous bicycle shop, and when three world-famous aviators (Octave Chanute, Samuel Langley and Otto Lilienthal) made various flight tests in 1896, the Wrights were inspired to build their first gliders.

Between 1899 and 1901, Wilbur and Orville visited Kitty Hawk, testing and developing their glider, and from 1902 to 1903 they built a powered aircraft. Their first powered flight took place on 17 December 1903: Orville flew 37 metres in 12 seconds and the momentous event was captured by Coast Guard John T. Daniels, who took a photograph of Orville in flight.

In 1907, the Wright brothers tried to sell their flyer in Europe and the US, but found that buyers wouldn't purchase an aircraft they hadn't seen fly. So, on 8 August 1908, Wilbur made his first public flight at Le Mans, France. That same year, Wilbur won the Michelin Cup and a prize of 20,000 francs for his flight of 123.2 kilometres, which lasted 2 hours 18 minutes and 33.6 seconds.

1908 was also the year of Orville's terrible flying accident. However, he recovered to join Wilbur in Paris the following year with his sister, Katharine. The three became international celebrities, meeting royalty and world leaders. In 1909, the Wright brothers received the Congressional Medal of Honor for their contribution to flight and were guests of honour at a grand homecoming celebration in Dayton. They finally secured contracts to sell their machine to the US military, and to top off a great year, Wilbur's 33-minute flight up and down the Hudson River was witnessed by one million New Yorkers, cementing their fame in America.

On 25 May 1910, Orville piloted two unique flights: the first, with Wilbur as his passenger (the only time their father allowed the brothers to fly together), and the second, with his 82-year-old father. This was the only flight of Milton Wright's life, and as the aircraft rose to 350 feet (107 metres), he was said to have shouted, "Higher, Orville, higher!"

On 30 May 1912, Wilbur Wright died at the early age of 45 at home, in Dayton Ohio, surrounded by his family. Orville went on to become president of the Wright Company and continued to work in aviation, taking his last ever flight on 19 April 1944. Orville joked that the wingspan of the Lockheed Constellation in which he sat was longer than the distance of his first flight!

Many contest whether the Wright brothers were truly first to fly; indeed, many other aviators took to the air around the same time as the Wrights. Nevertheless, their indisputable contribution to flight was the creation of a machine that could be consistently controlled and that could fly under its own power.

Orville Wright was born in the age of the horse-drawn carriage, and he grew old enough to see the birth of jet planes and supersonic flight. The Wright brother's passion and mechanical innovation inspired others to push the technology of flight forwards, dawning a new age of air travel.

*To Wilbur, Orville, and all who dedicated*
*their lives to the pursuit of flight — A.H.*

**Quarto** Knows

Quarto is the authority on a wide range of topics.

Quarto educates, entertains and enriches the lives of our readers—enthusiasts and lovers of hands-on living.

www.quartoknows.com

First published in Great Britain in 2017 by Frances Lincoln Children's Books,
The Old Brewery, 6 Blundell Street, London, N7 9BH
QuartoKnows.com · Visit our blogs at QuartoKnows.com

A catalogue record for this book is available from the British Library.

This book is not produced or licensed by the The Wright Brothers Family Foundation.

ISBN 978-1-84780-928-5

Published by Rachel Williams · Edited by Jenny Broom
Designed by Nicola Price · Production by Dawn Cameron

Printed in China

3 5 7 9 8 6 4 2

MIX
Paper from
responsible sources
FSC® C104723
www.fsc.org

Photographic acknowledgements (pages 30–31, clockwise from top) 1. Orville Wright, 1874 © Library of Congress 2. Wilbur Wright, 1876 © Library
of Congress, Getty Images 3. Test Flight of Wright Glider, 1902 © Library of Congress, Getty Images 4. Wright Brothers National Memorial ©
Moelyn Photos, Getty Images 5. Orville, Wilbur and Katharine Wright, 1900 © Bettmann, Getty Images